A SESAME STREET BOOK

The Sesame Street Players Present

Mother Goose

Illustrated by Michael J. Smollin

On the tape that accompanies this Storybook, the performer is: CAROLL SPINNEY — Big Bird

Distributed by Tyco® in cooperation with Children's Television Workshop expressly for Big Bird® Story Magic.® Initially published by Random House
© 1986 Children's Television Workshop. © 1986 Jim Henson Productions, Inc. All rights reserved. No part of this book may be reproduced or copied
in any form without written permission. Sesame Street and the Sesame Street Sign are trademarks and service marks of Children's Television
Workshop. Mfd. by Tyco Industries, Inc., Moorestown, NJ 08057.
PRINTED IN KOREA

Rub-a-dub-dub,
Three men in a tub,
And who do you think they be?
The butcher, the baker,
The candlestick maker;
Turn 'em out, knaves all three!

Star light, star bright,
First star I see tonight,
I wish I may, I wish I might,
Have the wish I wish tonight.

Mary had a little lamb,
Its fleece was white as snow;
And everywhere that Mary went
The lamb was sure to go.
It followed her to school one day,
That was against the rule;
It made the children laugh and play
To see a lamb at school.
And so the teacher turned it out,
But still it lingered near,
And waited patiently about
Till Mary did appear.
Why does the lamb love Mary so?
The eager children cry;
Why, Mary loves the lamb, you know,
The teacher did reply.

Rain on the green grass,
And rain on the tree,
Rain on the housetop,
But not on me.

Twinkle, twinkle, little star,
How I wonder what you are!
Up above the world so high,
Like a diamond in the sky.
Twinkle, twinkle, little star,
How I wonder what you are!

Little Boy Blue,
Come blow your horn,
The sheep's in the meadow,
The cow's in the corn.
Where is the boy
Who looks after the sheep?
He's under a haystack
Fast asleep.
Will you wake him?
No, not I,
For if I do,
He's sure to cry.

It's raining, it's pouring,
The old man's snoring;
He got into bed
And bumped his head
And couldn't get up in the morning.

Wee Willie Winkie runs
Through the town,
Upstairs and downstairs
In his nightgown,
Rapping at the window,
Crying through the lock,
Are the children all in bed,
For now it's eight o'clock.

Humpty Dumpty sat on a wall,
Humpty Dumpty had a great fall;
All the King's horses and all the King's men
Couldn't put Humpty together again.

If all the world were paper,
And all the sea were ink,
If all the trees were bread and cheese,
What should we have to drink?

Three young rats with black felt hats,
Three young ducks with white straw flats,
Three young dogs with curling tails,
Three young cats with demiveils,
Went out to walk with three young pigs
In satin vests and sorrel wigs;
But suddenly it chanced to rain,
And so they all went home again.

Who made the pie?
I did.
Who stole the pie?
He did.
Who found the pie?
She did.
Who ate the pie?
You did.
Who cried for pie?
We all did.

Sing a song of sixpence,
A pocket full of rye;
Four-and-twenty blackbirds
Baked in a pie!

When the pie was opened,
The birds began to sing;
Wasn't that a dainty dish
To set before the King?

Pat-a-cake, pat-a-cake, baker's man,
Bake me a cake as fast as you can;
Pat it and prick it, and mark it with B,
Put it in the oven for baby and me.

Old Mother Hubbard
Went to the cupboard
To fetch her poor dog a bone;
But when she came there
The cupboard was bare
And so the poor dog had none.

"Pussy-cat, pussy-cat,
Where have you been?"
"I've been to London
To look at the Queen."
"Pussy-cat, pussy-cat,
What did you there?"
"I frightened a little mouse
Under the chair."

Monday's child is fair of face,
Tuesday's child is full of grace,
Wednesday's child is full of woe,
Thursday's child has far to go,

Friday's child is loving and giving,
Saturday's child works hard for its living,
But the child that's born on the Sabbath day
Is bonny and blithe, and good and gay.

Little Jack Horner
Sat in the corner,
Eating his Christmas pie;
He put in his thumb
And pulled out a plum
And said, What a good boy am I!

Old Farmer Giles,
He went seven miles
With his faithful dog Old Rover;
And Old Farmer Giles,
When he came to the stiles,
Took a run, and jumped clean over.

Rain, rain, go away,
Come again another day;
Little Johnny wants to play.

Little Bo-Peep has lost her sheep
And doesn't know where to find them;
Leave them alone, and they'll come home,
Bringing their tails behind them.

Little Bo-Peep fell fast asleep
And dreamed she heard them bleating;
But when she awoke, she found it a joke,
For they were still a-fleeting.

Then up she took her little crook,
Determined for to find them;
She found them indeed, but it made her heart bleed,
For they'd left their tails behind them.

5¢ PIES

Simple Simon met a pieman,
Going to the fair;
Says Simple Simon to the pieman,
"Let me taste your ware."

Says the pieman to Simple Simon,
"Show me first your penny;"
Says Simple Simon to the pieman,
"Indeed, I have not any."

Higglety, pigglety, pop!
The dog has eaten the mop;
The pig's in a hurry,
The cat's in a flurry,
Higglety, pigglety, pop!

If all the seas were one sea,
What a great sea that would be!
If all the trees were one tree,
What a great tree that would be!
And if all the axes were one axe,
What a great axe that would be!
And if all the men were one man,
What a great man that would be!
And if the great man took the great axe,
And cut down the great tree,
And let it fall into the great sea,
What a splish-splash that would be!

Hickory, dickory, dock!
The mouse ran up the clock;
The clock struck one,
And down he run,
Hickory, dickory, dock!

Sally go round the sun,
Sally go round the moon,
Sally go round the chimney pots
On a Saturday afternoon.

Ride a cock-horse to Banbury Cross,
To see a fine lady upon a white horse;
Rings on her fingers and bells on her toes,
And she shall have music wherever she goes.

Hey, diddle, diddle!
The cat and the fiddle,
The cow jumped over the moon;
The little dog laughed
To see such sport,
And the dish ran away with the spoon.

One, two, three, four, five,
Once I caught a fish alive,
Six, seven, eight, nine, ten,
Then I let it go again.
Why did you let it go?
Because it bit my finger so.
Which finger did it bite?
The little finger on the right.

Little Miss Muffet
Sat on a tuffet,
Eating her curds and whey;
There came a big spider,
Who sat down beside her
And frightened Miss Muffet away.

I love little pussy,
Her coat is so warm,
And if I don't hurt her,
She'll do me no harm.
So I'll not pull her tail,
Nor drive her away,
But pussy and I
Very gently will play.
She shall sit by my side,
And I'll give her some food;
And pussy will love me
Because I am good.

Jack and Jill went up the hill,
To fetch a pail of water;
Jack fell down, and broke his crown,
And Jill came tumbling after.

Jack Sprat could eat no fat,
His wife could eat no lean,
And so between them both, you see,
They licked the platter clean.

Three wise men of Gotham
Went to sea in a bowl;
If the bowl had been stronger,
My story would have been longer.

Jack be nimble,
Jack be quick,
Jack jump over
The candlestick.

Go to bed late,
Stay very small;
Go to bed early,
Grow very tall.

To market, to market,
To buy a plum bun;
Home again, home again,
Market is done.

Old King Cole
Was a merry old soul,
And a merry old soul was he;

He called for his pipe,
And he called for his bowl,
And he called for his fiddlers three!

Cock a doodle doo!
My dame has lost her shoe,
My master's lost his fiddling stick
And knows not what to do.

Cock a doodle doo!
My dame has found her shoe,
And master's found his fiddling stick
Sing doodle doodle doo.

Cock a doodle doo!
What is my dame to do?
Till my master finds his fiddling stick
She'll dance without her shoe.

Cock a doodle doo!
My dame will dance with you,
While master fiddles his fiddling stick
For dame and doodle doo.

This little pig went to market;
This little pig stayed at home;
This little pig had roast beef;
This little pig had none;
This little pig cried,
"Wee, wee, wee!" all the way home.